How to Conquer the World on a Shoestring Budget

How To Conquer The World, Volume 1

Æ Æ

Published by Æ, 2023.

HOW TO CONQUER THE WORLD ON A SHOESTRING BUDGET

First edition. June 14, 2023.

ISBN: 979-8223836766

Written by Æ Æ.

Also by Æ Æ

How To Conquer The World
How to Conquer the World on a Shoestring Budget

Table of Contents

Intro

Welcome, dear reader, to the whimsical and satirical world of "How to Conquer the World on a Shoestring Budget." In these pages, we embark on a tongue-in-cheek journey filled with laughter, sarcasm, and ingenious thrifty tactics that may or may not lead to world domination.

Now, you might be wondering, can one truly conquer the world on a shoestring budget? Is it possible to achieve global domination without breaking the bank? Well, prepare yourself for a delightful exploration of these absurd possibilities.

In this book, we invite you to set aside your conventional thinking and join us on a hilarious adventure where common sense is thrown out the window, and resourcefulness reigns supreme. We'll tackle the challenges of ruling on a tight budget, strategize conquests with rubber bands and cardboard tanks, and discover the art of haggling your way to world dominance.

But let's be clear: this book is not meant to be a serious guide for would-be dictators or conquerors. Instead, it's a playful exploration of what might happen if we took thriftiness to the extreme and let our imaginations run wild. It's an invitation to embrace humor, satire, and a touch of absurdity as we navigate the world of conquering on a shoestring.

Throughout these pages, you'll find witty stories, sarcastic anecdotes, and practical(ly impractical) tips that challenge the norms of traditional conquest. From budget-friendly espionage techniques to building a formidable arsenal with household items, we'll leave no stone unturned (unless it's a discounted stone, of course).

But amidst the humor and sarcasm, there's a deeper message: to find joy in the simple pleasures, to embrace our creative instincts, and to question the norms that govern our lives. It's a reminder that a tight budget should never dampen our spirits or limit our ambitions.

So, grab your sense of humor, sharpen your wit, and prepare to embark on a hilarious and satirical journey through the chapters of this book. Whether you're seeking a good laugh or a dose of inspiration for your own thrifty adventures, we're delighted to have you join us.

Remember, dear reader, the world may not be conquered with spare change and stolen airline peanuts, but a clever mind, a dash of resourcefulness, and a healthy dose of laughter can take us on an unforgettable adventure.

Are you ready to conquer the world on a shoestring budget? Let the laughter begin!

Chapter 1: Unleashing Your Inner Cheapskate

Penny-Pinching Power

Once upon a time in the small town of Thriftyville, there lived a notorious cheapskate named Mildred. She was known far and wide for her unmatched ability to pinch pennies, squeeze nickels, and stretch every dollar to its breaking point. Her frugality was legendary, and her savings account was the envy of all who knew her.

Mildred was born with a natural knack for thriftiness. Even as a child, she would meticulously collect spare change from the couch cushions and trade her lunchbox snacks for leftover classroom supplies. While other kids dreamt of candy and toys, Mildred's eyes twinkled at the prospect of saving those precious pennies.

As she grew older, Mildred's penny-pinching prowess only strengthened. She became a master of coupon-clipping, scouring newspapers and magazines for discounts on everything from groceries to haircuts. She wouldn't hesitate to haggle with shopkeepers, armed with her secret weapon: an arsenal of well-researched competitor prices.

Mildred's friends often marveled at her thriftiness, simultaneously amused and amazed at her ability to turn even the most mundane activities into cost-saving adventures. Whether it was reusing tea bags for a second steep or meticulously planning her routes to maximize gas mileage, Mildred was always one step ahead of everyone else.

Her reputation as a cheapskate grew to such heights that the town even honored her with the title of "The Grand Frugalmeister," complete with a golden coupon-shaped trophy. Mildred would proudly display it on her mantelpiece, a reminder of her triumphs in the realm of frugality.

But Mildred's penny-pinching power extended beyond her own personal savings. She saw it as a duty to share her wisdom with others and help them unleash their inner cheapskates. She organized workshops on DIY household cleaners, teaching attendees how to make their own laundry detergent from leftover soap scraps and baking soda.

In the evenings, Mildred would host frugal feasts at her humble abode, where friends and neighbors gathered to savor simple yet delicious meals prepared from discounted ingredients. She delighted in showing them that a feast fit for a king could be enjoyed on a shoestring budget.

As the years went by, Mildred's influence spread far and wide. People from neighboring towns sought her advice on thrifty living, and she became a local celebrity. Newspaper articles were written about her ingenious money-saving strategies, and television crews flocked to capture her frugal escapades.

But amidst all the fame and recognition, Mildred remained humble and true to her cheapskate roots. She knew that true power lay not in extravagant spending but in the ability to make every dollar count. Her message was simple: by embracing our inner cheapskate, we can free ourselves from the shackles of mindless consumerism and find joy in the art of saving.

And so, dear reader, as you embark on your journey through the chapters of this book, remember the tale of Mildred, the unstoppable force of frugality. Embrace your inner cheapskate, let your creative juices flow, and discover the immense satisfaction that comes from taming your spending habits.

The Art of Bargaining: How to Negotiate Like a Pro (or at Least Like a Thrifty Dictator)

Once upon a time, in the land of thrifty conquerors and discount dictators, there lived a shrewd and sly ruler named Dictator Chester the Cheap. He was renowned throughout the kingdom for his remarkable ability to negotiate anything, from the price of a goat to the cost of a kingdom-sized moat, all while maintaining his iron-fisted rule.

One fine day, Dictator Chester embarked on a mission to the local market in search of a rare and majestic unicorn. Rumor had it that a vendor named Honest Abe possessed the most extraordinary unicorns at the most exorbitant prices. Determined to prove his frugal finesse, the dictator donned his finest robe made entirely of stitched-together discount coupons and set off on his quest for thrifty triumph.

As Dictator Chester approached Honest Abe's stall, he was met by a pompous man with a mustache so bushy it could easily house a family of squirrels. The vendor boasted about the mythical powers of his unicorns and began quoting a price that would make even the wealthiest of dictators hesitate.

But Dictator Chester was no ordinary ruler. He had mastered the art of bargaining to such an extent that even the most stubborn salespeople would crumble under his thrifty might. With a sly smirk on his face and a tone of mock enthusiasm, he initiated his negotiation strategy.

"Well, well, Honest Abe," Dictator Chester began, his voice dripping with sarcasm. "I've heard tales of your magnificent unicorns, but I'm afraid your asking price is more elusive than the unicorns themselves. Surely, a thrifty dictator like myself could never dream of affording such an extravagant creature."

Honest Abe puffed out his chest, attempting to maintain an air of superiority. "My unicorns are worth every ounce of gold, Your Dictatorship. They possess the ability to grant immortality and bring eternal prosperity to your regime."

The dictator leaned in closer, his voice filled with faux curiosity. "Immortality, you say? How intriguing. But tell me, Honest Abe, do these unicorns also come with a lifetime supply of discounted unicorn feed and a coupon for magical veterinarian visits? After all, I wouldn't want my precious unicorns draining the treasury."

The vendor's confidence faltered as he realized he was dealing with a master bargainer. "Well, perhaps we can find a compromise," he mumbled, his mustache quivering under the pressure.

Dictator Chester seized the opportunity, employing every trick in the thrifty negotiator's playbook. He scrutinized every inch of the unicorn, pointing out imaginary flaws, and argued for a "slightly imperfect goods" discount. He haggled over the delivery fee, insisting that unicorns should be capable of trotting themselves to their new dictator's domain.

Finally, after what felt like an eternity of cunning banter, Dictator Chester emerged triumphant. Not only had he secured a price far below Honest Abe's initial offer, but he had also negotiated a lifetime supply of rainbow-colored hay for his prized unicorn.

As the dictator rode triumphantly back to his palace on the back of his newly acquired budget-friendly unicorn, he couldn't help but chuckle at the fortune he had saved. He was a true master of negotiation, a legend among the thrifty, and a beacon of hope for every budget-conscious dictator in the land.

From that day forward, Dictator Chester the Cheap was revered not only for his iron-fisted rule but also for his unparalleled ability to negotiate like a pro. His regime thrived, not because of opulent wealth, but due to the power of a clever remark and an unwavering commitment to securing the best deal.

And so, dear reader, the moral of this tale is simple: In the realm of bargaining, where discounts and deals reign supreme, even the most cunning of dictators can conquer the world on a shoestring budget. Just remember, a sharp tongue and a relentless pursuit of savings are all you need to negotiate your way to thrifty domination.

Dumpster Diving 101: Unearthing Hidden Treasures on a Budget

Once upon a time, in a world where treasure could be found amidst trash and junk, there lived a peculiar group of individuals known as the Dumpster Diving Daredevils. These intrepid adventurers embraced the art of dumpster diving with unmatched enthusiasm, seeking to unearth hidden treasures on a shoestring budget.

Our story begins with Penny, a self-proclaimed dumpster diving aficionado. Armed with a headlamp and a trusty pair of gloves, Penny embarked on a midnight mission to a nearby supermarket dumpster, known to be a goldmine of discarded goodies.

As Penny approached the towering dumpster, the scent of expired yogurts and stale bagels filled the air. Undeterred by the less-than-pleasant fragrance, she dove headfirst into the world of dumpster delights.

With nimble fingers and a keen eye, Penny rummaged through the discarded produce, day-old donuts, and partially squashed soda cans. The sight would make most people gag, but not Penny. No, she saw potential where others saw rubbish.

And lo and behold, after mere moments of digging through the sea of discarded items, Penny's gloved hands struck gold. Well, not literally gold, but close enough—a slightly dented can of beans that had expired only a week ago. Triumphantly, she added it to her growing collection of dumpster treasures.

As Penny continued her expedition, she stumbled upon a discarded lamp missing its lampshade. Undeterred by its lack of aesthetic appeal, she saw an opportunity to create a quirky conversation piece for her living room. With a little duct tape and a lot of imagination, she proudly displayed her "Dumpster Chic" lamp for all to see.

But Penny's dumpster diving adventures didn't stop there. Oh no, she was just getting started. She ventured into dumpsters behind clothing stores, emerging triumphantly with fashionably mismatched socks and slightly wrinkled shirts that only required a bit of ironing to look presentable.

Word of Penny's dumpster diving prowess spread throughout the town, attracting a motley crew of fellow treasure hunters. They formed the Dumpster Diving Daredevils, sharing tips, tricks, and tales of their most outrageous finds.

One day, as the Daredevils explored a dumpster behind an electronics store, they stumbled upon a discarded, slightly cracked smartphone. With a bit of technical wizardry and a generous application of duct tape (their favorite tool), they managed to revive the phone, proclaiming it the ultimate symbol of their dumpster diving conquests.

The Daredevils became local legends, their unconventional lifestyle celebrated by the community. People marveled at their ability to turn trash into treasures, to find beauty in the discarded and value in the forgotten.

And so, dear reader, the moral of this whimsical tale is clear: In the realm of dumpster diving, where the unexpected can become extraordinary, there is a whole world of hidden treasures waiting to be discovered. With a pinch of resourcefulness, a dash of humor, and a lot of gloves, one can navigate the dumpsters of life, unearthing gems amidst the garbage and embracing the hilarity of finding fortune on a shoestring budget.

Haggling Your Way to World Domination: Crushing the Competition with Discounted Deals

Once upon a time, in a land where cutthroat business tactics and discount warfare ruled supreme, there lived a crafty and relentless entrepreneur named Larry the Haggler. Larry had a grand vision: he wanted to conquer the world, not with an army of soldiers, but with his unbeatable haggling skills and a stash of discounted deals.

Armed with a pocketful of coupons and a charismatic smile, Larry set out on his quest for global domination. His first target was the ruthless multinational corporation known as MegaCorp. This colossal company had a stranglehold on the market, but Larry was undeterred. He knew that in the realm of discounted deals, no empire was invincible.

Larry entered MegaCorp's luxurious headquarters, wearing his finest suit made entirely of stitched-together price tags. He approached the CEO's office, ready to engage in a battle of wits and bargaining. The secretary eyed him suspiciously, clearly unimpressed by Larry's thrifty attire.

"I demand to see your CEO," Larry declared with an air of faux importance. "I have a proposition that will revolutionize your business and save you a fortune in the process."

After a brief standoff with the secretary, Larry was finally granted an audience with the CEO, Mr. Monopoly Man. The room was filled with expensive artwork and plush furniture, symbols of MegaCorp's opulence. Larry couldn't help but suppress a chuckle. Little did they know what he had up his sleeve—or rather, in his discount-filled pockets.

Larry began his pitch, using every ounce of his sarcasm-laden charm. "Mr. Monopoly Man, I have a proposition that will make your competitors quake in their designer boots. Imagine, if you will, a world where every product in your empire is acquired at a fraction of the cost. A world where you crush the competition not with brute force, but with discounted deals so irresistible that customers flock to you like seagulls to a french fry."

Mr. Monopoly Man raised an eyebrow, clearly intrigued yet skeptical. "And how, pray tell, do you plan to accomplish such a feat?"

Larry grinned, his eyes gleaming with mischief. "Through the power of haggling, my dear sir. I will negotiate with suppliers, vendors, and anyone else who stands in our way, securing deals so mind-blowingly cheap that even the most frugal of penny-pinchers will bow before us."

The CEO leaned back in his plush chair, stroking his imaginary beard. "I must admit, your audacity is intriguing, young Haggler. But why should I entrust you with such a monumental task?"

Larry's sarcasm-filled response came naturally. "Because, Mr. Monopoly Man, in a world filled with inflated egos and overpriced commodities, I am the master of negotiation. I can turn a thousand dollars into a million, a discount into a dynasty. With my guidance, MegaCorp will become an unstoppable force, ruling the business world on a shoestring budget."

The CEO was visibly impressed. He extended his hand, a sign of reluctant admiration. "Very well, Larry the Haggler. You have piqued my interest. Show me what you can do."

And so, Larry set off on his mission, haggling his way through the labyrinthine corridors of the business world. He negotiated discounts on raw materials, slashed advertising costs, and even convinced rival companies to merge under the banner of MegaCorp, all while maintaining his sarcastic wit and trademark charm.

With each successful deal, MegaCorp's power grew, and Larry's reputation as the Haggler of World Domination spread far and wide. Competitors trembled at the mere mention of his name, knowing that their extravagant empires were no match for his thrifty tactics.

And so, dear reader, the moral of this tale is simple: In the realm of business, where profit margins reign supreme, it is the crafty and sarcastic hagglers who hold the keys to world domination. With a quick tongue, a sly smile, and an unwavering commitment to discounted deals, one can crush the competition and conquer the world, all while saving a few bucks along the way.

The Thrifty Traveler's Guide: Exploring the World on a Shoestring Budget (Hint: Couchsurfing and Stolen Airline Peanuts)

Once upon a time, in a world where wanderlust met frugality, there lived a traveler extraordinaire named Thrifty Terry. Terry had a burning desire to explore the world, but his budget was as tight as a pair of skinny jeans after Thanksgiving dinner. Undeterred by financial limitations, he embarked on a journey to become the most thrifty and resourceful globetrotter the world had ever seen.

Terry's first weapon of choice in his quest for cheap travel was Couchsurfing. Armed with his trusty sleeping bag and a charming smile, he hopped from one stranger's couch to another, leaving a trail of gratitude and faint potato chip crumbs in his wake. Why spend money on fancy hotels when you can experience the authentic joy of sleeping on a lumpy sofa, right?

But Terry's thrifty adventures didn't stop there. Oh no, he had another trick up his well-worn sleeve. As he boarded airplanes, Terry would stealthily snatch as many bags of airline peanuts as his nimble fingers could grab. He saw it as a survival technique, a way to sustain himself during long flights without spending a dime on overpriced snacks. Plus, he reasoned, he was doing the airline a favor by lightening their load. Talk about a win-win!

As Terry trotted the globe, he encountered fellow travelers who marveled at his thrifty tactics. They couldn't believe he could afford to see the world on such a shoestring budget. He proudly shared his wisdom, regaling them with tales of his Couchsurfing conquests and his peanut-poaching prowess.

One fateful day, Terry found himself in a bustling market in Marrakech. The aromas of exotic spices and haggling filled the air. It was a bargain hunter's paradise, and Terry's thrifty senses tingled with excitement. He joined the chaotic dance of bartering, wielding his sarcasm and wit like a sword, ready to conquer any vendor who dared overcharge.

As he negotiated with a vendor over a vibrant rug, Terry pulled out his secret weapon: a tattered copy of "The Art of Haggling for Dummies." Armed with its quirky tips and sarcastic suggestions, he dazzled the vendor with his knowledge of bargaining techniques. The price dropped lower and lower, leaving the vendor bewildered and Terry feeling like the Sultan of Savings.

With his trusty rug in tow and his pockets filled with stolen peanuts, Terry continued his global escapades. From climbing ancient ruins to sampling street food delicacies, he embraced every adventure with a thrifty gusto that would make even the most frugal soul proud.

And so, dear reader, the moral of this amusing tale is clear: In the realm of travel, where wanderlust meets financial limitations, it is the clever and sarcastic thrifty travelers like Terry who truly conquer the world. With Couchsurfing as their trusty steed and stolen airline peanuts as their sustenance, they navigate the globe on a shoestring budget, proving that you don't need a hefty wallet to experience the wonders of the world.

Chapter 2: Warfare for the budget consciousness minded ruler

Frugal Armies and Budget Battles: Conquering Without Breaking the Bank"

Once upon a time in the land of Cheaptopia, there existed a fearless and frugal leader named General Cornelius Cheapwise. He was known far and wide for his strategic brilliance and unmatched ability to conquer territories without breaking the bank. His army, aptly named the Frugal Forces, was a unique blend of resourcefulness and determination.

General Cheapwise had always believed that true power lay not in extravagant weaponry or opulent displays of wealth, but in the ability to outwit and outmaneuver the enemy using limited resources. He saw warfare as a battle of wits and ingenuity, where the victor was not the one with the biggest budget, but the one with the thriftiest tactics.

General Cheapwise's army was comprised of soldiers who embraced the art of frugality. They were trained to make do with whatever they had, whether it was fashioning makeshift armor from discarded soda cans or repurposing household items as weapons. Their battle cry echoed through the battlefield, "Save money, conquer the world!"

In their conquests, General Cheapwise and his Frugal Forces relied on strategic planning and cunning maneuvers rather than brute force. They would study the enemy's weaknesses and exploit them, using diversionary tactics and ambushes to gain the upper hand. While other armies marched with expensive weaponry, the Frugal Forces marched with rubber band slingshots and catapults made from popsicle sticks.

The general understood that communication was key in warfare, but traditional methods of messaging were costly. So, he devised a clever system of sending secret messages using recycled paper and homemade ink made from beetroot. His messages were passed through the ranks swiftly and discreetly, ensuring that the enemy remained oblivious to their plans.

But perhaps the most impressive display of frugal warfare came during the Battle of Thrifty Hill. The enemy had a massive fortress guarded by a moat filled with crocodiles, and it seemed impossible to breach their defenses. However, General Cheapwise had a trick up his sleeve. Instead of constructing expensive siege towers or employing costly mercenaries, he ordered his soldiers to build a makeshift bridge using fallen tree trunks and discarded ropes. With their combined strength and determination, they crossed the moat, surprising the enemy and swiftly taking control of the fortress.

News of General Cheapwise's frugal conquests spread far and wide, and other leaders began to take note. They realized that victory could be achieved without bankrupting their kingdoms. The art of frugal warfare became a popular topic of discussion in military academies, and generals from all corners of the world sought to emulate General Cheapwise's tactics.

And so, dear reader, as you delve into the chapters of this book, remember the tale of General Cornelius Cheapwise and his Frugal Forces. Learn from their thrifty strategies, embrace the power of resourcefulness, and discover that victory can be attained without breaking the bank.

DIY Weapons: Crafting a Formidable Arsenal from Household Items (Who Needs Guns When You Have Rubber Bands?)

Once upon a time, in a world where creativity and resourcefulness reigned supreme, there lived a peculiar inventor named MacGyver McSpark. MacGyver had an uncanny ability to turn everyday household items into formidable weapons. Who needs guns when you have rubber bands, right? Armed with his trusty Swiss Army knife and a collection of rubber bands, MacGyver set out on a mission to prove that DIY weapons were the key to survival.

One fateful day, MacGyver found himself in a sticky situation. He was trapped in a room with a ferocious guard dog blocking his path to freedom. Most people would panic or cower in fear, but not MacGyver. Oh no, he saw this as an opportunity to put his DIY weapon skills to the test.

With a sly grin, MacGyver rummaged through his pockets and pulled out a handful of rubber bands. He knew that these humble elastic wonders held immense power. As the guard dog lunged at him, MacGyver swiftly stretched a rubber band between his fingers and let it fly. The rubber band struck the dog's snout, causing it to yelp and retreat in confusion. It seemed that even man's best friend was no match for the wrath of a well-aimed rubber band.

Emboldened by his victory, MacGyver continued his quest to demonstrate the might of DIY weapons. He transformed paperclips into lock-picking tools, turning locked doors into mere obstacles to be conquered. He fashioned a slingshot from a coat hanger and a rubber band, proving that ammunition need not be expensive when you have a good aim and a creative mind.

But MacGyver's DIY weapon arsenal didn't stop there. He crafted an improvised catapult out of spoons and rubber bands, launching small projectiles with surprising accuracy. He even fashioned a formidable boomerang out of a sturdy plastic plate and rubber bands, causing onlookers to marvel at his ingenuity.

As news of MacGyver's unconventional weapons spread, he found himself in high demand. People from all walks of life sought his expertise in turning the mundane into the extraordinary. From disgruntled office workers defending their cubicles with rubber band crossbows to parents using homemade water balloon launchers to settle disputes among siblings, MacGyver had become the guru of DIY weaponry.

And so, dear reader, the moral of this witty tale is crystal clear: In a world filled with expensive firearms and flashy gadgets, it is the sarcastic and inventive souls like MacGyver McSpark who prove that DIY weapons can pack a punch. So next time you find yourself in a sticky situation, remember to look around your house, grab some rubber bands, and unleash your inner MacGyver. Who knows, you might just find that the power to conquer lies in the most unexpected places.

Thrifty Tactics: The Art of Strategic Retreats and Budget-Savvy Sabotage

Once upon a time, in a world where being thrifty was a badge of honor, there existed a mischievous strategist named Pennywise Pete. Pete was a master of thrifty tactics, always finding creative ways to retreat strategically and sabotage on a shoestring budget. Armed with a pocketful of pennies and a devious grin, he embarked on his mission to outwit his adversaries and save a few bucks in the process.

Pennywise Pete's first encounter took place on the battlefield of a water balloon fight. As the enemy team unleashed a barrage of balloons, Pete quickly realized that his team was outgunned. But did he back down? Absolutely not! With a sly wink, he grabbed a handful of water balloons and retreated with a strategic retreat worthy of Sun Tzu himself. While his teammates floundered in the battle, Pete devised a plan to turn the tide in their favor without spending a fortune on water balloons.

Under the cover of darkness, Pennywise Pete sneaked into the enemy camp armed with a bucket of ice-cold water. He strategically placed it right above their makeshift fort, patiently waiting for morning to break. As the sun rose, the heat caused the ice to melt, drenching the enemy team in a surprise attack they never saw coming. Pete's thrifty tactic of using the elements saved his team from certain defeat, all without breaking the bank.

But Pennywise Pete's thrifty adventures didn't stop at water balloon fights. Oh no, he had a knack for budget-savvy sabotage as well. One day, he found himself in a high-stakes board game tournament, facing off against the craftiest opponents money could buy. Knowing he couldn't match their extravagant strategies, Pete devised a plan to level the playing field.

As the game progressed, Pennywise Pete unleashed his thrifty brilliance. He subtly hid a handful of Monopoly money in his pocket, ready to swap it with the real cash at the opportune moment. When his opponents least expected it, he skillfully maneuvered the game, pretending to hand over large sums of cash while slipping them counterfeit bills from his secret stash. His rivals, blinded by their own greed, were none the wiser. Pennywise Pete's thrifty sabotage had not only saved him money but had ensured his victory.

Word of Pete's thrifty tactics spread far and wide. People marveled at his ability to retreat strategically and sabotage with a limited budget. He became a legend, sought after by those who craved victory without draining their wallets. Pennywise Pete's thrifty teachings inspired a new generation of strategists who realized that winning wasn't about spending the most money, but about using wit, creativity, and a healthy dose of sarcasm to outsmart their opponents.

And so, dear reader, the moral of this tale is clear: In a world obsessed with flashy strategies and expensive tactics, it is the witty and thrifty souls like Pennywise Pete who reign supreme. So, the next time you find yourself in a battle, whether it be a water balloon fight or a high-stakes board game, remember that the art of strategic retreats and budget-savvy sabotage can be your secret weapon. After all, why break the bank when you can break your opponent's spirit with a well-placed penny?

Recruitment on a Budget: Assembling an Army of Discounted Desperados (Craigslist Mercenaries, Anyone?)

Once upon a time, in a world where budget constraints ruled the land, there was a cunning leader named Frugal Fred. Fred had a burning desire to conquer new territories, but his bank account resembled a desert devoid of funds. Undeterred by financial limitations, he embarked on a mission to assemble an army of discounted desperados. He knew that with the right blend of thriftiness and audacity, he could create a formidable force without breaking the bank.

Fred's first stop on his quest for budget-friendly mercenaries was the depths of the internet—Craigslist. Armed with his trusty mouse and a cup of lukewarm coffee, he perused the classifieds section in search of warriors willing to join his cause for a fraction of the usual price. "Mercenaries wanted: Must be experienced in budget battles, and the ability to conquer on a shoestring budget is a plus!" he posted, hoping to attract the attention of frugal fighters.

To his surprise, responses poured in faster than he could count his pennies. Desperate job seekers and adventure enthusiasts alike flocked to his cause, eager to join an army that promised both excitement and a discounted paycheck. Fred conducted interviews in coffee shops, carefully assessing each candidate's ability to haggle, think outside the box, and maintain a sense of humor in the face of adversity. It was no ordinary army he was assembling; it was a ragtag band of penny-pinching warriors ready to conquer the world.

With his newfound recruits, Fred set out on his conquest. Armed with shoestring bows, recycled shields, and swords forged from discounted scrap metal, they marched forward, ready to face any adversary that stood in their way. The enemy forces scoffed at their budget equipment, underestimating the power of a determined heart and an eye for a good deal.

As they battled their way through treacherous terrain, Fred's army showcased their thrifty prowess. They used coupon codes to negotiate surrender from opposing forces. They strategically deployed BOGO deals to confuse their foes.

And in the face of scarcity, they resorted to guerrilla tactics, ambushing their adversaries with an onslaught of discounted merchandise and clearance aisle distractions.

Word of Fred's discounted desperados spread far and wide. Merchants trembled at the sight of their frugal army, for they knew that even the mightiest fortress could crumble under the weight of a well-timed 50% off sale. Fred's budget army became a force to be reckoned with, not because of their extravagant resources, but because of their sheer determination and thrifty strategies.

And so, dear reader, the moral of this amusing tale is crystal clear: In a world of exorbitant costs and inflated prices, it is the witty and resourceful leaders like Frugal Fred who assemble the most formidable armies. So, the next time you find yourself in need of an army, don't despair over a lack of funds. Embrace your inner thrifty genius, recruit from Craigslist, and remember that a discounted desperado can be just as deadly as a well-funded soldier. After all, why spend a fortune on mercenaries when you can conquer the world with a few savvy bargains and a dash of sarcasm?

From Cardboard Tanks to Peashooter Cannons: Unleashing the Power of Cost-Effective Warfare

Once upon a time, in a world where creativity met resourcefulness, there lived a wily strategist named Crafty Carl. Carl had a passion for warfare, but his pockets were as empty as a politician's promises. Undeterred by his lack of funds, he embarked on a mission to unleash the power of cost-effective warfare. Armed with cardboard tanks and peashooter cannons, he aimed to prove that victory could be achieved on a shoestring budget.

Carl's journey began in his own backyard, where he gathered a team of eager recruits who were just as penniless as he was. With rolls of duct tape, stacks of cardboard, and a pocketful of spare change, they set out to create a formidable army. They transformed cardboard boxes into armored tanks, complete with makeshift turrets and painted-on camouflage. Their peashooter cannons consisted of repurposed PVC pipes, rubber bands, and, of course, a generous supply of peashooter ammunition.

Their first battle took place in an abandoned field, pitting Carl's ragtag army against a heavily equipped foe. The enemy forces laughed heartily at the sight of the cardboard tanks and peashooter cannons, considering them nothing more than a comical sideshow. Little did they know, Crafty Carl had a few thrifty tricks up his sleeve.

As the battle commenced, Carl's army strategically maneuvered their cardboard tanks, surprising the enemy with their agility and durability. The peashooter cannons unleashed a barrage of projectiles, hitting enemy soldiers square in the face with peas of fury. The enemy's laughter quickly turned to confusion, as they realized that they were being outmaneuvered and outgunned by a group of crafty warriors armed with nothing more than cardboard and legumes.

Carl's army embraced their underdog status and unleashed a series of cost-effective tactics that left their opponents dumbfounded. They utilized decoy cardboard tanks to distract the enemy, while their stealthy soldiers snuck up from behind, armed with super soakers filled with water balloons. The enemy forces were drenched, defeated, and thoroughly embarrassed.

News of Crafty Carl's cost-effective warfare spread like wildfire. Soon, people from all walks of life sought his thrifty wisdom. DIY enthusiasts transformed their living rooms into battlegrounds, constructing cardboard fortresses and perfecting their aim with homemade slingshots. Craft stores experienced a sudden surge in demand for cardboard and rubber bands, as citizens armed themselves with the tools of frugal warfare.

And so, dear reader, the moral of this tale is clear: In a world where military might often depends on deep pockets and fancy gadgets, it is the clever and resourceful souls like Crafty Carl who prove that cost-effective warfare can be just as effective, if not more so. So, the next time you find yourself in a battle, whether it be a water fight with friends or a friendly cardboard tank skirmish, remember that victory can be achieved with a touch of creativity, a pinch of sarcasm, and a wallet that remains intact. After all, who needs expensive weapons when you can conquer the world armed with little more than cardboard tanks and peashooter cannons?

Chapter 3: Frugality in overdrive

Thriftiness on the Throne: Ruling with a Tight Fist and an Empty Wallet

Once upon a time, in the land of Pinchpenny, there reigned a king with a peculiar name: Frugal Ferdinand. King Ferdinand was known far and wide for his obsession with thriftiness. He believed that ruling with a tight fist and an empty wallet was not only possible but necessary to maintain a prosperous kingdom. Thus, he embarked on a reign that would leave his subjects both amused and bewildered.

King Ferdinand's first order of business was to scrutinize the royal budget with the precision of a miserly accountant. He slashed expenses left and right, banishing any unnecessary luxuries from the kingdom. Golden chalices were replaced with tarnished mugs, and feasts fit for royalty were substituted with humble peasant fare. The royal treasury breathed a sigh of relief, as it no longer had to bear the weight of exorbitant expenditures.

To showcase his commitment to thriftiness, King Ferdinand hosted a grand banquet, inviting guests from neighboring kingdoms. Expecting a lavish affair, the guests were greeted with a sight they would never forget. The banquet hall was adorned with secondhand decorations, held together by duct tape and sheer determination. The feast consisted of leftover bread and soup made from scraps. The guests, initially shocked, soon found themselves chuckling at the king's audacity.

But King Ferdinand's thriftiness did not stop at banquets. Oh no, he extended it to every aspect of his rule. He abolished unnecessary taxes, citing the kingdom's need to save every last copper coin. He encouraged his subjects to recycle and reuse, promoting a culture of thriftiness and environmental responsibility. The royal court was filled with eccentric characters who wore patched clothing and bragged about their ability to squeeze every last drop out of a bar of soap.

While some viewed King Ferdinand's frugality as eccentricity, others admired his dedication to wise spending. The kingdom thrived under his rule, as resources were allocated with precision and excess was avoided at all costs. The subjects learned to make the most out of what they had, finding joy in thriftiness and the art of repurposing.

One day, a neighboring king arrived at King Ferdinand's court, baffled by the tales he had heard. He challenged King Ferdinand, claiming that ruling with an empty wallet was impossible. King Ferdinand, ever the thrifty ruler, proposed a wager. They would compete in a series of challenges, from crafting the cheapest crown to organizing the most cost-effective parade. The neighboring king, fueled by pride, accepted the challenge.

The kingdom buzzed with excitement as the challenges unfolded. King Ferdinand, armed with creativity and a knack for finding bargains, outshone his rival at every turn. His crown, made from recycled bottle caps, shone brighter than any jewel-encrusted headpiece. His parade, filled with creatively repurposed floats and enthusiastic peasants, captured the hearts of the onlookers.

In the end, King Ferdinand emerged victorious, proving that ruling with a tight fist and an empty wallet was not only possible but could lead to a kingdom filled with resourcefulness, laughter, and prosperity. The neighboring king, humbled by his defeat, returned to his own kingdom, inspired by the thrifty tactics he had witnessed.

And so, dear reader, the moral of this story is as clear as a clearance sale sign: In a world where excess and wastefulness often rule the day, it is the thrifty and resourceful leaders like King Ferdinand who leave a lasting impact. So, the next time you find yourself in a position of power, remember that ruling with a tight fist and an empty wallet can lead to a kingdom where thriftiness reigns and laughter echoes through the halls. After all, who needs opulence when you can rule with a dose of humor and a savvy approach to spending?

The Frugal Palace: Turning a Two-Bedroom Apartment into a Royal Residence

Once upon a time, in the bustling city of Thriftville, there lived a thrifty couple named Penny and Walter. They dreamed of living in a grand palace, but their bank account could barely afford a two-bedroom apartment. Undeterred by financial limitations, Penny and Walter set out on a mission to transform their humble abode into a regal residence fit for a king and queen, all on a shoestring budget.

They began by scouring thrift stores and garage sales, searching for treasures that would elevate their living space to new heights of frugal luxury. Armed with paintbrushes and a bucket of mismatched paint cans, they set to work transforming their walls from drab to fab. They cleverly mixed colors, creating a royal palette of hues that would make any monarch envious.

The couple's creativity knew no bounds. They repurposed old furniture, transforming worn-out chairs into elegant thrones and outdated dressers into opulent cabinets. With a bit of DIY magic and some crafty ingenuity, their apartment was soon filled with regal accents and touches of extravagance—all acquired at bargain prices.

Penny and Walter knew that a palace is not complete without lavish textiles. But instead of splurging on expensive fabrics, they scoured discount stores for discounted curtains, elegant tablecloths, and sumptuous throw pillows. Their home became a tapestry of opulence, woven from the threads of thriftiness and their knack for finding bargains.

To add a touch of grandeur to their living space, Penny and Walter turned to the power of illusion. They strategically placed mirrors throughout the apartment, creating an illusion of spaciousness and grand halls. Their guests marveled at the seemingly endless rooms and corridors, unaware of the thrifty trickery that lay behind the reflection.

Of course, no frugal palace would be complete without a majestic dining experience. Penny and Walter transformed their modest kitchen into a culinary haven, armed with recipes that stretched every penny. They hosted grand feasts on a budget, concocting gourmet dishes from simple ingredients and adding a dash of creativity to every recipe. Their guests dined like royalty, unaware that the lavish banquet before them was the product of a frugal mastermind.

News of Penny and Walter's frugal palace spread throughout Thriftville, captivating the imaginations of its residents. Soon, people from all walks of life flocked to their apartment, seeking inspiration on how to transform their own humble dwellings into regal abodes. Penny and Walter, ever generous with their thrifty wisdom, shared their secrets with a smile and a hint of sarcasm.

And so, dear reader, the moral of this amusing tale is clear: In a world where opulence is often equated with wealth, it is the thrifty souls like Penny and Walter who prove that a frugal palace can be just as magnificent. So, the next time you find yourself dreaming of grandeur, remember that a two-bedroom apartment can be transformed into a royal residence with a dash of creativity, a knack for finding bargains, and a healthy dose of thriftiness. After all, who needs a fortune when you can live like a king or queen on a shoestring budget?

Taxation Techniques: How to Squeeze Every Last Penny from Your Loyal Subjects

Once upon a time, in the kingdom of Thriftopia, there reigned a ruler known as Taxmaster Tim. Tim had a unique talent for extracting every last penny from his loyal subjects. With a mischievous twinkle in his eye and a penchant for cunning, he devised taxation techniques that were both inventive and, some might say, diabolical.

Tim's first taxation technique was known as the "Air Tax." Believing that the very act of breathing was a privilege, he imposed a tax on every breath taken by his subjects. Each exhale came with a hefty price tag, leaving the people gasping for air both figuratively and literally. They soon realized that holding their breath wasn't just a survival technique but also a way to save a few precious coins.

Not content with just taxing the air, Taxmaster Tim introduced the "Sunshine Tax." He claimed that basking in the warm glow of sunlight was a luxury that warranted a fee. Every citizen who dared to enjoy the golden rays had to pay a tax proportional to the brightness of the day. The people reluctantly retreated to the shade, forever cursing the sun for its costly radiance.

But Taxmaster Tim's taxation techniques didn't stop there. He introduced the "Raindrop Tax," insisting that each raindrop that touched the ground carried a financial burden. Umbrellas became a prized possession, not for their ability to shield from the rain, but for their potential to catch every falling droplet and save a few precious coins. The people wandered the streets like juggling performers, deftly maneuvering their umbrellas to maximize their savings.

As if the air, sunshine, and rain weren't enough, Taxmaster Tim devised the most audacious taxation technique of all—the "Laughter Levy." He argued that laughter brought joy and happiness, which were clearly signs of financial prosperity. Thus, he implemented a tax on every hearty chuckle and every gleeful giggle. The kingdom fell into an eerie silence as the people guarded their lips, fearing the cost of a moment's mirth.

The people of Thriftopia, burdened by Taxmaster Tim's relentless taxation, became a resourceful bunch. They mastered the art of suppressed laughter, honing their skills to maintain a neutral expression while secretly reveling in the absurdity of it all. Laughter clubs formed in hidden corners, where suppressed chuckles could be released in safety, away from the prying eyes of tax collectors.

Word of Taxmaster Tim's taxation techniques spread to neighboring kingdoms, and rulers everywhere marveled at his audacity. Some applauded his ingenuity, while others shook their heads in disbelief. But one thing was clear—Taxmaster Tim had created a kingdom where every last penny was squeezed from his loyal subjects, leaving them with empty pockets and stifled laughter.

And so, dear reader, the moral of this tale is as sharp as Taxmaster Tim's tax collector's pen: In a world where taxation can sometimes feel burdensome, it is the witty souls like Taxmaster Tim who remind us of the importance of moderation and fairness. So, the next time you encounter a taxing situation, remember to approach it with a touch of humor, a pinch of sarcasm, and a strong urge to revolt. After all, who needs a kingdom filled with penniless subjects and stifled laughter when you can embrace a system that balances the need for revenue with the well-being of the people?

Budget Propaganda: Spreading Your Influence on a Shoestring Budget (Memes and Cat Videos for the Masses)

Once upon a time, in the digital realm of Frugalia, there existed a savvy ruler named Budget Baroness Beatrice. Beatrice understood that spreading influence and shaping public opinion didn't have to come with a hefty price tag. Armed with her wit, a keen understanding of human psychology, and an internet connection, she embarked on a mission to conquer hearts and minds on a shoestring budget.

Beatrice's weapon of choice? Budget propaganda. She recognized the power of memes and cat videos in capturing the attention of the masses. With a mischievous grin and a knack for comedic timing, she unleashed a wave of viral content that would make even the mightiest influencers envious.

Her first masterpiece was a meme that showcased a regal feline sporting a crown, accompanied by a witty caption: "When you're ruling the world on a shoestring budget but still look fabulous." The image spread like wildfire across social media platforms, capturing the hearts of cat lovers and budget-conscious individuals alike. It became a symbol of Frugalia's resilience and resourcefulness.

Not stopping there, Beatrice assembled a team of frugal content creators, armed with smartphones and a knack for creating viral videos. They crafted hilarious sketches featuring Frugalia's rulers engaging in everyday activities, all while promoting the benefits of living within one's means. The videos went viral, garnering millions of views and inspiring people to embrace thriftiness with a chuckle.

But Beatrice didn't rely solely on humor to spread her influence. She understood the power of emotional storytelling. She commissioned talented writers to pen heartfelt narratives, highlighting the struggles and triumphs of everyday Frugalians. These stories tugged at the heartstrings of readers, fostering a sense of unity and encouraging empathy. The tales spread like wildfire, igniting a sense of community within the kingdom.

In a stroke of genius, Beatrice also tapped into the power of nostalgia. She resurrected iconic advertisements from the past, giving them a frugal twist. Classic jingles were transformed into catchy tunes celebrating the joy of thriftiness. The familiar tunes played on radios and streamed through speakers, reminding the people of Frugalia that a sense of frugality could be found even in the sweet melodies of their childhood.

As the budget propaganda machine roared on, Frugalia experienced a cultural shift. The masses embraced thriftiness as a virtue, proudly sharing memes, cat videos, and heartwarming stories with their friends and families. The kingdom's influence grew, not through opulent displays or extravagant campaigns, but through the power of wit, relatability, and a touch of silliness.

And so, dear reader, the moral of this whimsical tale is as clear as a viral video's view count: In a world where influence is often equated with grandeur and expense, it is the clever souls like Budget Baroness Beatrice who remind us of the power of humor, relatability, and emotional storytelling. So, the next time you seek to spread your influence on a shoestring budget, remember to embrace the magic of memes, cat videos, and a dash of nostalgia. After all, who needs an extravagant budget when you can conquer the hearts of the masses with a well-placed LOL and a cleverly captioned cat?

Royal Dining on a Dime: Feasting Like a King without Bankrupting the Kingdom

Once upon a time in the kingdom of Thriftopia, there reigned a ruler known as King Reginald the Resourceful. Despite ruling over a realm of limited resources, King Reginald was determined to feast like a king without bankrupting the kingdom. With a pinch of creativity, a dash of thriftiness, and a hunger for culinary excellence, he set out to revolutionize the concept of royal dining on a dime.

King Reginald's royal chefs were accustomed to working with lavish ingredients and extravagant feasts. However, under the king's new decree, they had to adapt their culinary skills to a more frugal approach. With a twinkle in his eye, King Reginald challenged them to create mouthwatering dishes using the simplest and most affordable ingredients.

The royal kitchen buzzed with excitement as the chefs experimented with ingenious recipes. They transformed humble vegetables into magnificent works of art, weaving flavors and textures that delighted the taste buds. A simple carrot became a regal crown, adorned with caramelized glaze, while a lowly potato became a royal coach, stuffed with a delectable mixture of herbs and spices.

To save costs without sacrificing flavor, the chefs ventured beyond the palace walls to forage for wild herbs and mushrooms. They discovered hidden treasures in the kingdom's forests, transforming them into culinary masterpieces that rivalled the most extravagant feasts. King Reginald's dining table became a showcase of nature's bounty, a testament to the power of resourcefulness and a nod to the kingdom's natural wealth.

The king's thrifty tactics extended beyond the ingredients. He revolutionized the concept of royal dining by introducing communal feasts. Rather than individual plates overflowing with expensive delicacies, long banquet tables were set up where everyone could gather and share a meal. This not only fostered a sense of unity among the kingdom's residents but also significantly reduced food waste and expenses.

As word of King Reginald's frugal feasts spread throughout the land, neighboring rulers became curious. They sent emissaries to witness this remarkable feat of culinary thriftiness. Kings and queens from far and wide marveled at the creative dishes that graced the royal table. They left inspired, determined to implement similar practices in their own kingdoms.

King Reginald's revolution in royal dining had a profound impact, not only on the kingdom's finances but also on the culture and mindset of its people. The citizens embraced a newfound appreciation for simplicity and resourcefulness, realizing that a feast fit for a king could be achieved without breaking the bank.

And so, dear reader, the moral of this frugal tale is as sumptuous as a royal feast on a dime: In a world where opulence often overshadows practicality, it is the clever minds like King Reginald's that remind us of the power of creativity, resourcefulness, and communal dining. So, the next time you sit down for a meal, remember that feasting like a king doesn't require a royal budget. With a little imagination and a pinch of thriftiness, you too can savor the delights of a regal dining experience without bankrupting your own kingdom.

Chapter 4: Destroying the competition with no cash

Subversive Savings: Undermining the Competition with Financial Wit

Once upon a time in the kingdom of Savvyville, there lived a shrewd entrepreneur named Savage Sandy. Sandy was known for her subversive savings tactics, using financial wit to undermine the competition and rise to the top of the business world. Armed with a sly smile and a mind sharper than a money clip, she set out on a quest to outsmart her rivals.

Savage Sandy's first target was her arch-nemesis, Baron Bigbucks, a pompous tycoon with pockets deeper than the Mariana Trench. Determined to chip away at Bigbucks' empire, Sandy employed a clever strategy. She used her wit and charm to forge alliances with suppliers, negotiating discounts and preferential pricing. By securing better deals, she cut costs and passed the savings onto her customers, drawing them away from Bigbucks' overpriced products.

But Sandy's subversive savings didn't stop there. She knew that marketing played a crucial role in gaining the upper hand. With a twinkle in her eye, she launched a series of witty and sarcastic ad campaigns that poked fun at Bigbucks' exorbitant prices. Her commercials featured clever jingles and catchy slogans like, "Why pay a fortune when you can save with Sandy?" The kingdom's residents couldn't resist her charm and flocked to her stores, leaving Bigbucks scratching his head in disbelief.

Not content with just luring customers away, Savage Sandy devised a plan to infiltrate Bigbucks' company. She hired a team of undercover accountants who delved into the depths of Bigbucks' financial records, exposing excessive spending and wasteful practices. Sandy turned this information into a scandalous exposé, causing Bigbucks' reputation to plummet faster than the value of a defunct cryptocurrency.

Sandy's subversive savings tactics even extended to industry events and conferences. Knowing that networking and exposure were key to success, she devised a plan to attend these gatherings without breaking the bank. Instead of splurging on expensive tickets and lavish accommodations, Sandy organized her own guerrilla networking events in nearby coffee shops and parks. Armed with business cards and a knack for charm, she made connections and sealed deals while sipping on a cup of budget-friendly joe.

As news of Savage Sandy's subversive savings tactics spread, other entrepreneurs and small businesses rallied behind her. They formed an alliance, united in their mission to disrupt the status quo and level the playing field against corporate giants. Together, they shared tips and tricks, forming a formidable network of financial wit that left the competition trembling in their expensive leather shoes.

And so, dear reader, the moral of this subversive tale is as crafty as Savage Sandy's savings tactics: In a world where big corporations often hold all the cards, it is the witty minds like Sandy's that remind us of the power of financial savvy, clever marketing, and a touch of rebellion. So, the next time you find yourself facing a Goliath in the business world, remember that with a dash of wit and a pinch of subversion, you too can undermine the competition, disrupt the norm, and carve out your own path to success.

Frugal Espionage: Spying on a Shoestring Budget (Hint: Binoculars Made from Toilet Paper Rolls)

In the clandestine world of espionage, where secrets are bought and sold like cheap knockoff watches, there lived a master spy named Agent Thrifty Tina. Tina was known for her frugal approach to espionage, always finding a way to gather valuable information on a shoestring budget. Armed with her wit, resourcefulness, and a pair of binoculars made from toilet paper rolls, she embarked on daring missions to uncover the truth.

One day, Tina received a top-secret assignment from her superiors: infiltrate an exclusive gala hosted by the mysterious Dr. Luxurius. This notorious billionaire was rumored to be involved in international money laundering, and Tina was determined to expose his illicit activities. However, there was one catch: her mission had to be conducted with minimal financial resources.

Undeterred by the challenge, Tina set her frugal espionage plan into motion. She knew that high-tech gadgets and fancy surveillance equipment were out of her budget, so she turned to her trusted toolkit of thrifty tricks. With a roll of duct tape, a couple of toilet paper rolls, and a magnifying glass from a novelty detective kit, she crafted her very own binoculars. While they may not have rivaled the precision of high-end optics, they were enough to get the job done.

Disguised as a janitor, Tina slipped into the gala unnoticed, armed with her homemade binoculars and a keen eye for detail. She mingled with the extravagant guests, listening attentively to their conversations while sipping on a glass of water (free of charge, of course). She strategically positioned herself near the dessert table, where she could eavesdrop on the whispers of the rich and powerful.

To gather even more valuable intelligence, Tina employed her frugal wit. She discreetly swapped out the memory card of a photographer's camera with a counterfeit one she had purchased for a fraction of the price. This allowed her to access confidential photos that held the key to Dr. Luxurius' clandestine activities.

As the night progressed, Tina stumbled upon an opportunity to access the host's private office. With a hairpin as her lock-picking tool, she skillfully bypassed the security system and entered the inner sanctum. There, she discovered a hidden safe filled with documents that exposed Dr. Luxurius' dark secrets. With a grin of triumph, Tina snapped photos of the incriminating evidence using her trusty smartphone, which she had acquired from a discount store.

With her mission accomplished and the truth in her possession, Agent Thrifty Tina quietly slipped away from the gala, leaving the unsuspecting guests none the wiser. She returned to her secret headquarters, where she meticulously analyzed the gathered intelligence. The information she had obtained would not only bring down Dr. Luxurius but also expose a web of corruption that reached far beyond the gala.

And so, dear reader, the moral of this frugal espionage tale is as sharp as Agent Thrifty Tina's wit: In a world of high-tech gadgets and expensive spy gear, it is the resourceful minds like Tina's that remind us of the power of frugality, ingenuity, and a roll of duct tape. So, the next time you find yourself needing to spy on a shoestring budget, remember that with a little creativity and a pair of binoculars made from toilet paper rolls, you too can uncover secrets and expose the truth without breaking the bank.

Economic Warfare: Bankrupting Rivals and Pillaging Their Piggy Banks

In the cutthroat world of economic warfare, where fortunes rise and fall like the stock market, there lived a cunning strategist named Baron Thriftington. Known for his ruthless tactics and ability to bankrupt rivals, Thriftington was the bane of his competitors' existence. With his trusty calculator in hand and a mischievous glint in his eye, he set out on a mission to pillage their piggy banks and leave them financially destitute.

Thriftington's first target was his arch-nemesis, Count Spendleton, a flamboyant tycoon with a taste for opulence. Determined to topple Spendleton's empire, Thriftington devised a wickedly clever plan. He would undercut his rival's prices by offering absurdly low deals that no customer could resist. With profit margins razor-thin, Thriftington relied on volume to make up for the meager profits. The kingdom's residents flocked to his stores, leaving Spendleton's extravagant boutiques deserted and collecting dust like forgotten trinkets.

But Thriftington's economic warfare didn't stop at competitive pricing. He knew that information was power in the business world. So, he enlisted a team of cunning spies to infiltrate Spendleton's company and gather vital intelligence. They dug through financial records, discovered hidden assets, and unearthed dubious accounting practices. Armed with this knowledge, Thriftington exposed Spendleton's financial chicanery to the kingdom's regulators, resulting in hefty fines and tarnishing his rival's reputation.

Proud of his victory, Thriftington turned his attention to other unsuspecting targets. He launched a relentless advertising campaign, bombarding the kingdom's airwaves with catchy jingles and eye-catching slogans like "Don't Let Your Wallet Weep, Shop with Thriftington's Cheap!" The ads were a hit, luring customers away from his competitors like a swarm of bargain-hungry bees.

But Thriftington's most audacious move came in the form of a hostile takeover. He set his sights on a struggling company, poised for bankruptcy. With a stroke of financial wizardry, he acquired their assets at a fraction of their value, injecting new life into his own empire. It was a masterstroke that left his rivals scratching their heads, wondering how he managed to turn their misfortune into his triumph.

As Thriftington continued his reign of economic warfare, his rivals grew wary. They scrambled to find counterstrategies, but his relentless pursuit of profit always seemed one step ahead. Like a merciless pirate plundering a treasure chest, Thriftington seized every opportunity, leaving his competition in financial ruins.

And so, dear reader, the moral of this tale of economic warfare is as sharp as Thriftington's business acumen: In a world where money reigns supreme, it is the cunning minds like his that remind us of the power of strategy, calculation, and seizing opportunities. So, the next time you find yourself facing fierce competition, remember that with a shrewd plan and a killer instinct for profit, you too can bankrupt rivals and pillage their piggy banks, leaving them in your financial wake.

The Discount Diplomat: Navigating International Relations without Splurging on Expensive Gifts

Once upon a time in the land of Diplomavia, there lived a savvy diplomat named Ambassador Savvy McThriftington. Known for his thrifty approach to international relations, McThriftington was determined to navigate the complex world of diplomacy without emptying the kingdom's coffers on extravagant gifts. With a charming smile and a knack for negotiation, he set out on a mission to establish strong diplomatic ties on a shoestring budget.

Ambassador McThriftington's first challenge was to build a relationship with the wealthy Kingdom of Luxuria, known for their opulent tastes and love for lavish gifts. However, McThriftington knew that his kingdom couldn't afford to compete in the realm of grandiose gestures. Instead, he relied on his wit and resourcefulness to find a way.

Drawing inspiration from the old saying, "It's the thought that counts," McThriftington set out to curate thoughtful and unique gifts that wouldn't break the bank. He scoured local markets for handcrafted trinkets, each with a story and cultural significance. From intricately woven baskets to delicately painted ceramics, he handpicked items that showcased his kingdom's heritage and captured the essence of Diplomavia's rich culture.

But McThriftington didn't stop there. He understood the power of personalized gestures, so he took the time to research the Luxurian customs and traditions. Armed with this knowledge, he tailored his diplomatic engagements to align with their preferences. He presented Luxurian officials with beautifully handwritten letters of friendship and respect, expressing his admiration for their kingdom's achievements. These thoughtful gestures touched the hearts of his Luxurian counterparts, forging a genuine connection between the two realms.

As McThriftington ventured further into the world of discount diplomacy, he encountered new challenges. In one instance, he was tasked with hosting a state dinner for a delegation from the Kingdom of Exquisitania, known for their refined tastes in cuisine. Knowing that his limited budget couldn't compete with Exquisitania's culinary extravagance, McThriftington got creative.

He enlisted the help of talented local chefs who could transform simple and affordable ingredients into culinary delights. With their expertise, he designed a menu that showcased the best of Diplomavian cuisine, using cost-effective ingredients elevated with clever culinary techniques. The Exquisitanian delegation was pleasantly surprised by the unique flavors and McThriftington's ability to create a memorable dining experience without draining the kingdom's treasury.

McThriftington's thrifty approach to diplomacy extended beyond gift-giving and fine dining. He mastered the art of utilizing digital communication and virtual meetings to foster connections across borders, saving both time and resources. With a click of a button, he engaged in video conferences, shared presentations, and conducted virtual cultural exchanges, all while minimizing travel expenses and reducing the kingdom's carbon footprint.

And so, dear reader, the moral of this discount diplomacy tale is as astute as Ambassador McThriftington's diplomatic maneuvers: In a world where extravagant gifts and lavish displays often dominate the realm of international relations, it is the resourceful minds like McThriftington's that remind us of the power of thoughtfulness, cultural understanding, and personal connections. So, the next time you find yourself facing diplomatic challenges, remember that with a touch of creativity and a pinch of frugality, you too can navigate the complex world of international relations without splurging on expensive gifts, forging genuine connections that transcend material wealth.

Budget Assassins: Eliminating Enemies with Frugality and Finesse (Death by Discounted Poison)

Once upon a time in the clandestine world of espionage, there existed a secret organization known as the Frugal Assassins. Led by their shrewd and penny-pinching leader, Agent Pennyworth Nickelton, this group of budget assassins specialized in eliminating enemies with frugality and finesse. They believed that a well-executed assassination didn't have to break the bank. In fact, they took pride in accomplishing their deadly missions with the utmost efficiency and minimal expenditure.

One fateful day, Agent Nickelton received an assignment to take down a high-profile target known as Count Valucrius, a corrupt nobleman with a penchant for opulence and a laundry list of enemies. Nickelton knew that the mission required a special touch of frugality, so he assembled his team of budget assassins to devise a cunning plan.

Their first task was to acquire a lethal poison. Instead of purchasing an expensive and traceable substance, the Frugal Assassins opted for a more budget-friendly approach. They concocted their own toxic blend using discount household chemicals, crafting a deadly potion that would leave no trace and save them a considerable sum of money.

Next came the challenge of gaining access to Count Valucrius' heavily guarded mansion. The Frugal Assassins couldn't afford state-of-the-art gadgets or a full-scale infiltration operation. Instead, they hatched a plan to disguise themselves as a group of door-to-door salespeople. Armed with a catalog of discounted products, they skillfully maneuvered their way past the guards, relying on charm and persuasive sales pitches to gain entry.

Once inside, Agent Nickelton and his team needed to find the opportune moment to administer the poison. They utilized their sharp observation skills and knowledge of the count's routine to identify the perfect time when he would be alone and vulnerable. With the precision of a surgeon, they discreetly contaminated his favorite bottle of expensive wine, ensuring that he would unknowingly drink his own demise.

As the count fell victim to the deadly brew, the Frugal Assassins swiftly made their exit, leaving no trace of their presence behind. The mission was a success, and Count Valucrius met his untimely demise without the kingdom's treasury taking a significant hit.

Agent Nickelton and his team continued to carry out their budget assassinations, perfecting their frugal methods with each mission. They utilized discounted disguises, repurposed everyday items as lethal weapons, and relied on inconspicuous transportation methods to remain under the radar.

Their reputation grew, and soon they became known as the deadliest assassins in the underworld, not for their expensive gadgets or ostentatious displays of power, but for their ability to eliminate targets with frugality and finesse. Their enemies trembled at the thought of facing the Budget Assassins, knowing that death could come in the form of a discount store-bought poison or an unexpected blow from a repurposed household object.

And so, dear reader, the moral of this tale of budget assassins is as sharp as Agent Nickelton's dagger: In a world where assassinations are often associated with extravagant weaponry and elaborate schemes, it is the resourceful minds like the Frugal Assassins' that remind us of the power of ingenuity, thriftiness, and a touch of deadly finesse. So, the next time you find yourself needing to eliminate an enemy, remember that sometimes the deadliest weapon is a bargain find, and a little creativity goes a long way in the art of assassination.

Chapter 5: No money down conquest

Global Conquest, Penny by Penny: Expanding Your Empire on a budget

Once upon a time in the realm of ambitious conquerors, there was a peculiar figure known as Pennywise the Magnificent. Unlike the extravagant and lavish rulers of the past, Pennywise had a unique approach to global conquest – one that involved expanding his empire on a shoestring budget, penny by penny.

With a heart full of thriftiness and a mind brimming with cunning strategies, Pennywise set out on his quest for world domination. His first step was to assemble a team of loyal and resourceful advisors, who were experts in maximizing every penny and stretching the kingdom's resources to their absolute limit.

Together, they devised a grand plan to expand their empire through calculated acquisitions of smaller territories. Instead of engaging in costly battles and full-scale invasions, Pennywise utilized his shrewd negotiating skills to strike deals with weaker nations on the brink of bankruptcy. He saw the potential in these struggling lands and offered them a lifeline, albeit with a tiny price tag attached.

Pennywise's empire grew steadily as he acquired one struggling kingdom after another, all while keeping a tight hold on his treasury. He would negotiate with the rulers, offering them the opportunity to retain their titles and positions of power in exchange for a nominal fee and a pledge of loyalty. The conquered rulers, desperate to escape financial ruin, readily accepted the offer.

To maintain control over his expanding empire without exhausting his limited resources, Pennywise introduced a series of cost-cutting measures. He implemented a rigorous austerity program, where luxuries were replaced with frugality. Golden thrones were substituted with humble wooden chairs, grand banquets were downsized to modest feasts, and opulent palaces were transformed into efficient administrative buildings.

Pennywise's budget-conscious mindset extended to his army as well. Instead of investing in expensive weapons and armor, he found innovative ways to equip his soldiers. He repurposed everyday household items, turning broomsticks into spears and kitchen pots into helmets. His army, though unconventional in appearance, proved to be a formidable force on the battlefield.

In addition to strategic acquisitions and cost-cutting measures, Pennywise leveraged the power of propaganda to solidify his rule. Using his wit and charm, he spread tales of his empire's greatness far and wide. He employed a team of talented artists to create captivating posters and witty slogans, enticing people to join his empire and support his vision of a penny-wise world order.

As Pennywise's empire grew, he faced challenges from neighboring kingdoms who underestimated his thrifty tactics. They scoffed at his frugality, believing that wealth and opulence were the keys to conquest. Little did they know that Pennywise's clever strategies and relentless focus on thriftiness were his greatest weapons.

With each conquered territory, Pennywise expanded his influence and his treasury. He became known as the master of frugal conquest, the ruler who built an empire penny by penny. His subjects admired his ability to stretch resources and admired his vision of a thrifty world where every penny was valued.

And so, dear reader, the tale of Pennywise the Magnificent reminds us that in the pursuit of global conquest, one need not succumb to extravagance and excessive spending. With cunning strategies, careful negotiation, and a relentless focus on thriftiness, even the smallest of budgets can lead to the grandest of empires. Penny by penny, kingdom by kingdom, the path to world domination is paved with frugality and an unyielding determination to conquer on a shoestring.

Thrifty Colonization: Acquiring New Territories without Spending a Cent

Once upon a time in the vast realm of global conquest, there lived a unique and resourceful ruler known as Emperor Thriftius. While other leaders indulged in costly expeditions and lavish conquests, Emperor Thriftius had a different approach to acquiring new territories – one that involved colonization without spending a single cent.

Emperor Thriftius was a master of thriftiness, always seeking opportunities to expand his empire without depleting his treasury. He knew that traditional colonization methods required vast resources and expensive expeditions, but he was determined to find a way to colonize on a shoestring budget.

His quest for thrifty colonization led him to a brilliant realization – he would focus on unclaimed and overlooked lands. While other empires fought over the grand territories, Emperor Thriftius set his sights on hidden gems and forgotten corners of the world. These lands were often dismissed as barren or uninhabitable, but he saw their potential.

With his team of budget-minded advisors, Emperor Thriftius devised a plan to transform these overlooked territories into thriving colonies. They utilized creative tactics and exploited loopholes in international agreements to stake their claim without spending a single cent. They found deserted islands, barren deserts, and remote mountain ranges that were of no interest to other empires and declared them as part of their ever-expanding realm.

To encourage settlement in these new colonies, Emperor Thriftius offered incentives to adventurous individuals who were willing to relocate. He promised them the opportunity to build a new life and reap the benefits of the colony's future prosperity. Word spread like wildfire, and soon people from all walks of life flocked to the colonies, eager to be a part of Emperor Thriftius' grand vision.

Emperor Thriftius ensured that the development of the colonies remained cost-effective. He encouraged self-sufficiency and resourcefulness among the colonists. They built their homes using local materials and repurposed discarded items, turning ruins into vibrant communities. They cultivated the land, growing their own food, and traded among themselves to meet their needs.

Emperor Thriftius also embraced sustainable practices in the colonies, harnessing natural resources and employing renewable energy solutions. He believed that a thrifty empire should not only be economically efficient but also environmentally conscious.

As the colonies prospered under Emperor Thriftius' frugal rule, neighboring empires began to take notice. They were baffled by his ability to expand his territory without spending exorbitant sums of money. Some dismissed it as luck, while others were intrigued by the cleverness of his methods.

Word of Emperor Thriftius' thrifty colonization spread far and wide, inspiring other leaders to reconsider their own extravagant conquests. The notion of acquiring new territories without breaking the bank became a topic of intrigue and discussion among the ruling elite.

Emperor Thriftius' colonies grew into bustling centers of trade and culture. They became known for their resourcefulness, resilience, and thriving economies. People marveled at the empire's ability to achieve so much with so little, proving that colonization could be accomplished without extravagant expenditures.

And so, dear reader, the story of Emperor Thriftius and his thrifty colonization reminds us that conquest doesn't always require a bottomless treasury. With ingenuity, creativity, and a keen eye for overlooked opportunities, one can expand their empire without spending a cent. In a world driven by excessive spending, Emperor Thriftius stood as a shining example of how thriftiness can lead to prosperous colonization and a truly formidable empire.

Budget-Friendly Annexation: Winning Over Neighboring Nations with Coupon Codes and Discounted Diplomacy

Once upon a time in the land of ambitious rulers and power-hungry leaders, there lived a unique and cunning sovereign known as King Bargainus. While others resorted to costly wars and aggressive tactics to annex neighboring nations, King Bargainus had a secret weapon up his frugal sleeve – budget-friendly annexation through the art of coupon codes and discounted diplomacy.

King Bargainus believed that conquest didn't have to come at a hefty price. With his trusted advisors, he devised a strategy to win over neighboring nations using the power of discounts, bargains, and diplomatic thriftiness. He understood that the key to annexation wasn't through force, but rather through smart negotiations and irresistible deals.

Armed with a stack of coupon codes and a knack for finding the best bargains, King Bargainus embarked on his quest to expand his kingdom. He would approach neighboring rulers with an offer they couldn't refuse, a deal that would save them money and secure their loyalty.

His diplomatic envoys would arrive at the doorsteps of these nations, armed with discount vouchers and a gift basket filled with samples of the kingdom's finest products. The envoys would eloquently present the benefits of joining forces with King Bargainus, highlighting the cost savings and economic advantages of their proposal.

Using his charismatic charm and thrifty rhetoric, King Bargainus would negotiate treaties that would benefit both parties. He would offer reduced trade tariffs, access to exclusive deals with his kingdom's merchants, and even shared defense agreements, all at a fraction of the cost that other rulers would demand.

To sweeten the deal, King Bargainus would throw in additional incentives. He would present neighboring rulers with coupon books filled with discounts for luxurious goods and services. From discounted royal banquets to half-priced horse-drawn carriages, these coupon books became the talk of the neighboring kingdoms.

The rulers, enticed by the prospect of saving money and bolstering their economies, would eagerly sign the annexation treaties. They saw the financial benefits of aligning with King Bargainus, and the allure of coupon codes and discounted diplomacy proved irresistible.

With each successful annexation, King Bargainus would add to his kingdom's wealth and influence. His thrifty approach allowed him to expand his realm without depleting the treasury or resorting to expensive military campaigns. The neighboring nations, now part of his kingdom, marveled at the financial savvy of their new ruler.

As word spread of King Bargainus' budget-friendly annexation methods, neighboring rulers became increasingly intrigued by his approach. They admired his ability to achieve expansion without draining the coffers and saw the potential for economic growth and stability under his rule.

The kingdom of King Bargainus flourished as the annexed nations integrated into the realm. The economies boomed, with merchants and consumers benefiting from the cross-border trade agreements and discounted deals. The kingdom became a shining example of how thriftiness and diplomatic finesse could pave the way to a prosperous and united land.

And so, dear reader, the tale of King Bargainus and his budget-friendly annexation serves as a reminder that conquest doesn't have to break the bank. With the right mix of negotiation skills, persuasive charm, and the strategic use of coupon codes and discounted diplomacy, even the most ambitious annexations can be achieved on a tight budget. King Bargainus proved that a ruler's financial savvy can be just as powerful as any army, and that the path to expansion is not always paved with gold but with clever bargains and frugal alliances.

World Domination for Introverts: Conquering from the Comfort of Your Own Couch (Online Gaming and Virtual Empires)

Once upon a time, in a world where introverts ruled the land of their own thoughts and comfortable solitude, there was a clever and unassuming introvert named Max. While others sought to conquer the world through grand displays of power and charisma, Max had a different plan in mind. He aimed to achieve world domination without ever leaving the cozy comfort of his own couch.

Max knew that the traditional path to world domination required extensive social interactions, networking, and commanding attention in large crowds. But as a true introvert, he preferred the company of his thoughts, a warm blanket, and a trusty gaming console.

Armed with his gaming skills and a vast knowledge of virtual realms, Max embarked on his quest for global supremacy. He understood that in this digital age, true power lay within the realms of online gaming and virtual empires.

Max created his alter ego, known as the Silent Strategist, and entered the virtual battlefield. With his quick reflexes, cunning tactics, and innate ability to anticipate his opponents' moves, he quickly rose through the ranks of the gaming community. Max didn't need a charismatic persona or a loud voice to command respect. He let his skills do the talking.

As he conquered virtual territories and built his online empire, Max realized that the virtual world mirrored the real world in many ways. He formed alliances with other introverted gamers, forming a tight-knit community of like-minded individuals who shared his vision of world domination from the comfort of their own couches.

Together, they strategized, coordinated attacks, and defended their territories against rival gamers. They used their introverted nature to their advantage, analyzing their opponents' weaknesses and exploiting them without ever leaving the safety of their virtual command centers.

Max understood that world domination wasn't just about conquering virtual realms; it was about influencing the real world through the power of the digital domain. He leveraged his virtual empire to spread his ideas, shaping public opinion, and influencing global events through online communities, forums, and social media platforms.

While others were busy attending high-profile meetings and public gatherings, Max orchestrated his empire's growth and influence from the comfort of his own couch. He didn't need expensive suits or flashy presentations. Instead, he relied on his digital prowess, analytical thinking, and the sheer force of his virtual armies.

As news of the Silent Strategist's virtual conquests spread, world leaders began to take notice. They marveled at Max's ability to shape opinions and mobilize virtual armies to influence real-world events. They recognized the power of introverted individuals who preferred the solitude of their own thoughts but possessed an uncanny ability to sway public sentiment.

Max's influence grew exponentially as more introverted individuals joined his cause, rallying behind his vision of world domination from the comfort of their own couches. Together, they formed a formidable force that no extroverted leader could match.

And so, dear reader, the tale of Max, the introverted mastermind, serves as a reminder that world domination can be achieved through unconventional means. In a world dominated by extroverted personalities, introverts have their own unique strengths that can be harnessed for global influence. Through the power of online gaming and virtual empires, introverts can conquer the world from the comfort of their own couches, proving that sometimes, the quietest voices have the loudest impact.

International Aid on a Shoestring: Buying Alliances and Influence with Pocket Change

Once upon a time, in a world of powerful nations and grand alliances, there was a peculiar leader named Baron Thriftsworth. While others believed that international aid required vast sums of money and grand gestures, Baron Thriftsworth knew the true secret to buying alliances and influence with nothing more than pocket change.

With his tattered coat and a few coins jingling in his pocket, Baron Thriftsworth set out to make his mark on the world stage. He understood that money wasn't the only currency of influence; sometimes, it was the art of frugality that held the greatest power.

Baron Thriftsworth knew that nations with limited resources often valued even the smallest contributions. He would visit struggling countries, armed with a handful of coins, and present them as tokens of his goodwill and friendship. While others scoffed at his seemingly meager offerings, the Baron knew that these small gestures held immense symbolic value.

In one impoverished nation, he visited a village struggling with a lack of clean drinking water. While other leaders promised grand water treatment facilities, Baron Thriftsworth approached the villagers with a humble gift—a box of water purification tablets. With a smile, he explained how these affordable tablets could transform their contaminated water into something safe to drink. The villagers, touched by his thoughtfulness and practicality, welcomed him as a trusted ally.

Baron Thriftsworth didn't stop at small gifts; he also utilized his frugal wit to create mutually beneficial trade agreements. Instead of offering extravagant aid packages, he proposed fair and balanced trade deals that would benefit both his own nation and the countries he sought to win over. These deals were carefully crafted to promote economic growth and self-sufficiency, rather than perpetuating dependency.

His unique approach to international aid garnered attention and admiration from leaders around the world. They marveled at his ability to achieve remarkable results with minimal financial investment. Baron Thriftsworth had mastered the art of using pocket change to buy alliances and influence, demonstrating that true power lies not in lavish displays of wealth, but in resourcefulness and shrewd negotiation.

Word of his success spread far and wide, and nations began to seek his assistance. They saw the value in partnering with someone who could stretch every penny to its maximum potential. Baron Thriftsworth became a trusted advisor, helping struggling nations develop their economies, improve healthcare systems, and combat poverty—all within the constraints of a shoestring budget.

As his influence grew, Baron Thriftsworth's approach to international aid revolutionized the way nations interacted with one another. They realized that it wasn't the size of the checkbook that mattered, but rather the sincerity of the gesture and the genuine desire to uplift and empower others.

And so, dear reader, the tale of Baron Thriftsworth serves as a reminder that international aid doesn't have to be about extravagant displays of wealth. By using pocket change strategically and approaching aid with genuine compassion and practicality, one can buy alliances and influence, and make a lasting impact on the world. Baron Thriftsworth showed us that true power lies in the ability to make a little go a long way, and that sometimes, it's the smallest gestures that have the biggest impact on the world stage.

Chapter 6: Leaving a Legacy on a Dime

Thrifty Legacy: Ensuring Your Empire's Prosperity for Generations to Come

Once upon a time, in a kingdom renowned for its frugality and resourcefulness, there was a wise ruler named Duchess Thriftiana. As she surveyed her vast empire, she knew that ensuring its prosperity for generations to come required more than just conquering new territories and accumulating wealth. It required a thrifty legacy.

Duchess Thriftiana understood that fortunes could be easily squandered if not managed wisely. She knew that her empire's prosperity relied not only on her own reign but on the wise decisions and frugal practices of her successors. And so, she set out to establish a thrifty legacy that would guide her empire towards everlasting financial stability.

Duchess Thriftiana called together the most brilliant minds in her kingdom—financial advisors, economists, and experts in frugality. They brainstormed and devised a comprehensive plan to ensure the empire's financial longevity. They established policies to curb wasteful spending, maximize resource utilization, and invest wisely in areas that would yield long-term benefits.

One of Duchess Thriftiana's key initiatives was to instill a sense of financial responsibility in future generations. She implemented a mandatory financial education program in schools, teaching young minds the importance of budgeting, saving, and investing. She knew that by equipping the youth with financial literacy, they would grow up to be responsible stewards of the empire's wealth.

Furthermore, Duchess Thriftiana encouraged entrepreneurship and innovation within her kingdom. She provided incentives and support for small businesses and startups, fostering an environment where frugal ideas and cost-effective solutions thrived. This not only created new avenues for economic growth but also ensured a diverse and resilient economy that could weather any financial storm.

In her quest for a thrifty legacy, Duchess Thriftiana also emphasized the importance of sustainable practices. She championed green initiatives and renewable energy sources, recognizing that protecting the environment was not only morally responsible but also financially sound. By reducing waste, conserving resources, and embracing eco-friendly technologies, the empire could minimize expenses and create a more sustainable future.

To further secure her empire's prosperity, Duchess Thriftiana established a sovereign wealth fund. This fund would invest surplus resources in diverse industries and global markets, generating additional income for the empire and safeguarding against economic uncertainties. The returns from these investments would be reinvested back into the kingdom, fueling its growth and prosperity for generations to come.

As Duchess Thriftiana's reign continued, her thrifty legacy took root. The people of her empire embraced the frugal mindset, realizing that wealth wasn't measured by extravagant displays but by financial stability, sustainable practices, and prudent decision-making.

Generations passed, and the empire thrived. The principles of thrift and financial responsibility became deeply ingrained in the culture and values of the kingdom. The empire's wealth grew steadily, ensuring the prosperity of its citizens and the preservation of its natural resources.

And so, dear reader, the tale of Duchess Thriftiana and her thrifty legacy teaches us that building an empire isn't just about conquering lands and accumulating riches. It's about establishing a foundation of financial stability, resourcefulness, and sustainability. By instilling these values in future generations, we can create a legacy that transcends time and ensures the enduring prosperity of our empires.

The Budget Dynasty: Securing Succession through Discounted Inheritance Laws and Affordable Monarchy

Once upon a time, in the realm of Frugalia, there existed a royal family known as the Pennywises. This thrifty dynasty had a unique approach to securing their succession and maintaining their wealth on a budget. They believed in the power of discounted inheritance laws and an affordable monarchy.

The reigning monarch, King Thriftus, was a shrewd ruler who understood the value of every penny. He knew that passing on the kingdom to his heirs could be a costly affair, with extravagant estates, jewels, and treasures being the norm in other royal families. But King Thriftus had a different plan.

He gathered his royal advisors, accountants, and lawyers to discuss a new approach to inheritance. They brainstormed creative ideas to ensure that the kingdom's wealth remained intact without breaking the bank. After many budget-friendly discussions, they devised a set of discounted inheritance laws.

The Pennywise dynasty introduced policies that limited the lavishness of inheritances. Instead of extravagant estates, they opted for cozy cottages. Precious jewels were replaced with affordable heirlooms, and valuable artifacts were substituted with homemade crafts. The Pennywises were determined to create a legacy based on financial prudence rather than ostentatious displays of wealth.

To further secure their succession on a budget, the Pennywises implemented an affordable monarchy. They avoided extravagant ceremonies and opulent lifestyles, instead opting for a modest royal existence. The king's throne was a simple, repurposed armchair, and the crown jewels were cleverly crafted from discounted costume jewelry.

In addition to their discounted inheritance laws and affordable monarchy, the Pennywises were also known for their wise investments and thrifty financial practices. They embraced the power of compound interest and invested their kingdom's resources in sustainable ventures that yielded long-term returns.

The Pennywises were loved by their subjects for their relatability and down-to-earth approach. They engaged in charitable acts on a budget, organizing food drives and affordable healthcare initiatives for their people. Their reign was marked by financial stability, and the kingdom flourished under their frugal leadership.

As generations passed, the Pennywise dynasty's thrifty mindset and discounted inheritance laws became deeply ingrained in the kingdom's traditions. The royal heirs learned the importance of wise financial management and continued the legacy of affordable monarchy and frugal practices.

And so, the story of the Budget Dynasty teaches us that wealth and succession can be secured without excessive spending. By embracing discounted inheritance laws, maintaining an affordable monarchy, and practicing wise financial management, a dynasty can thrive and pass on its legacy to future generations without bankrupting the kingdom.

In the realm of Frugalia, the Pennywise dynasty stands as a shining example of how a budget-conscious approach can lead to long-lasting success and financial prosperity. Their thrifty practices continue to inspire rulers and citizens alike to this day, reminding us that a dynasty's true wealth lies not in extravagant displays, but in the smart management of resources and the preservation of financial stability.

Philanthropy for the Thrifty: Building Your Legacy by Donating Slightly Used Socks and Half-Eaten Granola Bars

Once upon a time, in the land of Thriftopia, there lived a peculiar philanthropist named Baron Bargainheart. Known for his frugality and resourcefulness, Baron Bargainheart believed in giving back to the community in his own unique way—by donating slightly used socks and half-eaten granola bars.

Baron Bargainheart had a remarkable talent for finding bargains and stretching every penny. He scoured thrift stores, garage sales, and discount bins for the best deals on socks and snacks. But instead of hoarding his findings, he had a brilliant idea. He realized that even these seemingly insignificant items could make a difference in the lives of others.

With a heart full of frugal generosity, Baron Bargainheart established the Society of Slightly Used Socks and Half-Eaten Granola Bars. This philanthropic organization aimed to provide essential items to those in need, all while keeping costs to a minimum.

Baron Bargainheart's first act of philanthropy took place on a chilly winter day. He gathered his fellow thrifty enthusiasts and embarked on a mission to distribute slightly used socks to the homeless. The socks, freshly laundered and still in decent condition, brought warmth and comfort to those who had little to protect their feet from the cold.

The Baron's philanthropic efforts didn't stop there. He recognized that hunger was another pressing issue in the community. Armed with a collection of half-eaten granola bars, he organized a "Snack Share" event in the local park. People gathered, grateful for the sustenance that these humble treats provided. They savored each bite, knowing that even a small snack could make a difference in their day.

As word of Baron Bargainheart's philanthropy spread, more people were inspired to contribute. Thrifty individuals from all walks of life started donating their slightly used socks and half-eaten granola bars to the cause. The Society of Slightly Used Socks and Half-Eaten Granola Bars became a community effort, fueled by the collective desire to make a difference without breaking the bank.

The impact of Baron Bargainheart's philanthropy was far-reaching. It wasn't just about the material items; it was about the message of compassion, resourcefulness, and empathy for those less fortunate. The Society's motto, "Spreading Care One Sock and Snack at a Time," resonated with people, reminding them that even the smallest act of kindness could have a ripple effect.

Baron Bargainheart's legacy as a thrifty philanthropist lived on for generations. The Society of Slightly Used Socks and Half-Eaten Granola Bars continued its noble work, expanding its reach and finding innovative ways to help those in need. From organizing thrift swaps to repurposing gently worn clothing, they exemplified the spirit of philanthropy on a shoestring budget.

And so, in the land of Thriftopia, the story of Baron Bargainheart and his philanthropic endeavors reminds us that generosity knows no bounds, even for those with limited financial means. Through creativity, resourcefulness, and a willingness to give back in unconventional ways, we can make a meaningful impact on the lives of others and build a legacy of compassion, one slightly used sock and half-eaten granola bar at a time.

The Frugal Architect: Constructing Monumental Landmarks with Recycled Materials and Discounted Contractors

Once upon a time, in the enchanting realm of Frugalia, there lived a visionary architect named Stella Saversmith. Known far and wide as "The Frugal Architect," Stella had a remarkable talent for creating monumental landmarks on a shoestring budget. She was a master of resourcefulness, using recycled materials and discounted contractors to bring her grand visions to life.

Stella's journey as a frugal architect began when she stumbled upon a forgotten plot of land. While others saw it as an empty canvas, Stella saw potential. She realized that with a little creativity and a tight budget, she could transform this barren space into something extraordinary.

Armed with her trusty blueprint and a knack for finding incredible deals, Stella embarked on a mission to construct a landmark that would defy expectations. She scoured thrift stores, salvage yards, and construction site dumpsters in search of hidden treasures. She found reclaimed wood, salvaged bricks, and even repurposed window frames—all waiting to be transformed into architectural wonders.

With her recycled materials in hand, Stella needed the perfect team to bring her vision to life. She sought out contractors who were skilled but willing to work for a fraction of their usual fees. She became known for her ability to negotiate rock-bottom prices, using her charm and wit to convince talented craftsmen to join her budget-friendly endeavors.

Together, they embarked on their first project—a magnificent structure made entirely of repurposed shipping containers. Stella and her team worked tirelessly, transforming these discarded metal giants into a breathtaking work of art. What was once used to transport goods now became a stunning testament to creativity and frugality.

Word of Stella's architectural prowess spread like wildfire. People marveled at her ability to create awe-inspiring landmarks on a tight budget. Soon, individuals and communities from across Frugalia sought her out for their own projects. From sculptures made of recycled plastics to gardens adorned with repurposed tires, Stella's portfolio grew, each creation more unique and impressive than the last.

But Stella's mission went beyond just constructing remarkable landmarks. She believed in the power of sustainability and educating others about the importance of reusing and repurposing materials. She held workshops and seminars, sharing her frugal techniques with aspiring architects and enthusiasts alike. Stella's passion for thriftiness became contagious, inspiring others to think outside the box and embrace the beauty of recycled architecture.

As the years went by, Stella's legacy as the Frugal Architect grew. Her landmarks dotted the landscape of Frugalia, each one a testament to her ingenuity and determination. People from far and wide flocked to witness the magic of her recycled creations, marveling at how something so extraordinary could be born from humble beginnings.

And so, in the enchanting realm of Frugalia, the story of Stella Saversmith, the Frugal Architect, reminds us that great feats of architecture can be accomplished with resourcefulness, creativity, and a keen eye for a good deal. It shows us that beauty can be found in the discarded, and that even on a limited budget, we can create magnificent landmarks that inspire generations to come.

Thrifty Immortality: Becoming a Legend without Spending a Dime (Urban Legends and Penny-Saving Folklore)

In the small town of Pennyville, there lived a peculiar character named Sam Thriftwell. Sam was notorious for his frugal ways and his unwavering determination to become a legendary figure without spending a single dime. He believed that true immortality could be achieved through the power of urban legends and penny-saving folklore.

Sam's quest for thrifty immortality began one fateful evening when he stumbled upon an old book of local myths and legends. As he delved into its pages, he realized that these stories held the key to his immortality. With a mischievous grin, he set out to create his own tales of wonder and intrigue, all on a shoestring budget.

His first endeavor involved the legendary "Haunted Mansion on Penny Lane." Sam knew that a ghostly tale was sure to captivate the imaginations of the townsfolk. So, armed with a white sheet, some glow-in-the-dark paint, and his knack for theatrics, he transformed himself into the legendary Penny Lane Ghost. Sam would appear in the darkest hours, haunting the local cemetery and giving passersby a good scare. Soon, whispers of the ghostly apparition spread, and Sam's legend began to take shape.

But Sam didn't stop there. He knew that to achieve true thrifty immortality, he needed a tale that would stand the test of time. Inspired by ancient legends of hidden treasure, he concocted the story of the "Penny Pot of Gold." Sam scattered copper coins throughout the town, carefully planting them in the most unexpected places—a crack in the sidewalk, the hollow of a tree, even the bottom of a public fountain. He whispered to anyone who would listen about the secret fortune awaiting those who could find all the scattered pennies. As locals scoured the town, excitement grew, and the legend of the Penny Pot of Gold spread like wildfire.

Sam's thrifty immortality didn't stop at creating legends. He became a master storyteller, regaling anyone who would listen with tales of thriftiness and penny-saving prowess. He would gather around campfires, spinning yarns about frugal wizards who turned pennies into gold and tightfisted fairies who granted wishes in exchange for a single coin. His stories sparked the imaginations of young and old alike, inspiring them to embrace a thrifty lifestyle and seek their own path to immortality.

As the years went by, Sam's legend grew, and he became an integral part of Pennyville's folklore. His name became synonymous with thriftiness, and people would jestingly say, "As thrifty as Sam Thriftwell!" His tales of urban legends and penny-saving folklore became the stuff of local lore, passed down through the generations.

And so, in the quirky town of Pennyville, the story of Sam Thriftwell stands as a testament to the power of thrifty immortality. It reminds us that sometimes the greatest legends are not born from extravagant expenses, but from the cleverness and creativity of those who dare to embrace a frugal way of life. Sam Thriftwell, the master of urban legends and penny-saving folklore, became a legend himself, proving that true immortality can be achieved without spending a dime.

Afterword

And so, we come to the end of this hilarious and sarcastic journey through the pages of "How to Conquer the World on a Shoestring Budget." We hope you've had a laugh, gained some creative insights, and maybe even discovered a penny-pinching trick or two along the way.

Remember, this book is not meant to be a serious guide for world domination or conquest. It's a whimsical exploration of what could happen if thrifty tactics were taken to the extreme. The stories and chapters within these pages were crafted with a tongue-in-cheek approach, aiming to entertain and tickle your funny bone.

While we've delved into the realms of thriftiness, sarcasm, and absurdity, it's important to remember that responsible decision-making and ethical behavior should always guide our actions. The world may not be conquered with spare change or stolen airline peanuts, but the spirit of resourcefulness and creativity can certainly enhance our lives in meaningful ways.

So, as you close this book, we encourage you to take a lighthearted approach to life, embrace your inner thrifty conqueror, and find joy in the little things. Remember that a sense of humor can go a long way, especially when facing the challenges of our daily lives.

Thank you for joining us on this wild and witty adventure. May your world be filled with laughter, clever bargains, and a healthy dose of sarcasm. Now, go forth and conquer the world (or at least conquer your next budget-friendly adventure) with a twinkle in your eye and a penny in your pocket. Happy thrifty conquering!

About the Author

Introducing Æ, the enigmatic author of this book. While many authors proudly display their names on the cover, Æ has chosen to embrace the mystique of anonymity, for reasons that will soon become apparent. You see, Æ's vast knowledge and expertise in the realm of conquering the world on a shoestring budget have attracted the attention of some exceptionally thrifty warlords and penny-pinching dictators.

These frugal powerhouses, with their keen eye for savings and unwavering commitment to budgetary constraints, have become aware of Æ's ability to unravel their closely guarded secrets and expose their cost-effective strategies of global dominance.

In order to protect himself from the relentless pursuit of these frugal warlords, Æ has taken refuge in anonymity. Within the shadows, he dedicates himself to extensive research, writing, and crafting the witty and sarcastic tales you'll find within these pages. Æ's concealed identity allows him to fearlessly delve into the realm of thriftiness, offering invaluable insights without fear of retribution.

Don't miss out!

Visit the website below and you can sign up to receive emails whenever Æ Æ publishes a new book. There's no charge and no obligation.

https://books2read.com/r/B-A-EMYY-VYJKC

BOOKS 2 READ

Connecting independent readers to independent writers.

Also by Æ Æ

How To Conquer The World
How to Conquer the World on a Shoestring Budget